Copyright © 1997 by Timothy Roland
All rights reserved under International and Pan-American Copyright Conventions.
Published in the United States by Random House, Inc., New York,
and simultaneously in Canada by Random House of Canada Limited, Toronto.

http://www.randomhouse.com/

Library of Congress Cataloging-in-Publication Data
Roland, Timothy.
Come down now, flying cow! / by Timothy Roland.
 p. cm.
"Beginner Books."
SUMMARY: Curious to see outside her field, Beth the cow sneaks onto a hot air balloon
and goes for a wild ride, upsetting a number of people and collecting many objects
and additional riders along the way.
ISBN 0-679-88110-7 (trade). — ISBN 0-679-98110-1 (lib. bdg.)
[1. Hot air balloons—Fiction. 2. Cows—Fiction. 3. Stories in rhyme.]
I. Title. PZ8.3.R6557Co 1997 [E]—dc20 96-42560

Printed in the United States of America 10 9 8 7 6 5 4 3 2 1

COME DOWN NOW, FLYING COW!

by Timothy Roland

BEGINNER BOOKS   A Division of Random House, Inc.

I'm Beth the cow.
I want to see
outside my field.
Come fly with me!

I sneak on board.

I look around.

I drop the ropes.

"Not now," I say,
and wave good-bye.
There's lots to see.
So off we fly!

We float up high.

Wow! What a sight!

"Look out!" yells Bird.

"Don't hit that kite!"

"Stop!" screams the boy.

But on we go.

Bird points ahead

and yells, "Oh, no!"

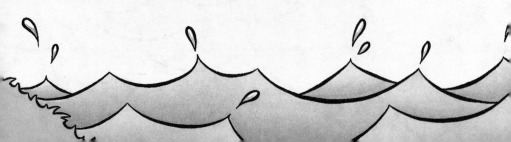

We drop down low.

A fish jumps high.

"Stop!" yells the man.
But off we fly.

We pass through clouds.

I drink some rain.

"Watch out!" yells Bird.

"Here comes a plane!"

HELP!

The plane loops up.

We hear a shout.

A lady and

her dog fall out.

We make a catch.

Down we go.

Now we're flying

very low.

We scrape a treetop,
roof, and gate.

"Look out!" yells Bird.

But it's too late!

Two women yell,
"Come down here, cow!
Bring back those clothes
and that dog—NOW!"

"Not now," I say.
"For we must fly
to where the buildings
touch the sky."

We bump a wall,
which scares a cat,
who drops a mouse
down on a hat.

A girl jumps up.
Her hat flies high.
"Come back!" she yells.
But on we fly.

We spot a game.

"A hit!" I shout.

I catch the ball.

The batter's out!

Bird turns around
and yells, "Oh, no!"
We're going down.
Look out below!

We hit.
We bump.
We land.
THUMP!
THUMP!

The people scream.
I don't know why
they frown at me
as they run by.

I turn around.

Who do I see?

It's Farmer Gray.

He's here for me.

"Don't fly again!"
yells Farmer Gray.
I look around,
then say, "Okay."

Next time I want
to travel far
outside my field...